A New Reindeer Friend

By Jessica Julius

Illustrated by the Disney Storybook Art Team

 A GOLDEN BOOK • NEW YORK

Princess Anna and Queen Elsa were working hard to prepare for the royal ball. The kingdom had accepted Elsa—and her magical powers—wholeheartedly, and the sisters wanted to thank the people with a special celebration.

"There you are, Elsa!" Anna exclaimed, bounding in with a tray of *krumkake*. "I haven't seen you all week!"

"I know! I've missed you," Elsa said.

"What do you think?" Elsa asked, nodding at the decorations. "I want the people of Arendelle to know we care. This ball should be something they'll always remember!"

"Simply *having* a ball is special," said Anna.

Just then, Gerda entered the room and looked around. "Crocus flowers would be nice for the centerpieces," the kind servant suggested.

"That's a lovely idea," Anna said. "But the party is tonight, Elsa. And you need a break. Besides, I want to spend time with you!"

"I'd love that, too," replied Elsa, thinking quickly. "So let's gather the crocuses ourselves! We'll do something useful *and* we'll be together."

Olaf waved as the sisters ran out of the castle.

"Hi, Anna! Hi, Elsa! Where are you going?"

"We're going to look for crocuses," called Anna.

"Oooh! That's one of my favorite flowers!" Olaf shouted.

Anna, Elsa, and Olaf
hiked into the mountains
and played together all day.

"Maybe our party should be a costume ball!" Anna said, giggling after putting a snowy beard on Elsa's face.

"I almost forgot about the ball!" Elsa cried. "We still need to find some crocuses."

As they made their way over the mountain, Anna spotted Wandering Oaken's Trading Post & Sauna.

"I remember this place," said Anna. "I bet Oaken will have something unusual for our ball." She ran inside, pulling Elsa along behind her.

"Hoo-hoo!" called Oaken as the girls entered the trading post.

"Hello! Do you have anything special for a ball?" asked Anna.

"My big winter blowout special is going on!" Oaken exclaimed. "Half off shoes for walking on snow! Or carts for sliding down mountains!"

Back outside, Elsa laughed as Anna pulled the cart and snowshoes behind her. "We already did the winter-in-summer thing, remember?"

Anna grinned. "I know, but he was so nice—how could I say no?"

Just then, Olaf noticed a bunch of beautiful crocuses!

The girls collected flowers as Olaf happily chased a bee.
All was going well until . . .

. . . Olaf got too close to a cliff's edge.

"Hang on, there, Olaf!" exclaimed Elsa,
catching the snowman right before he tumbled.

But Olaf didn't even notice he had been in danger.
"Look at that!" he said, pointing to a baby reindeer
stranded on a ledge.

"How did you get down there?" Anna asked the
reindeer. "And how will we get you up here?"

Elsa thought for a moment.
Then she waved her hands. Suddenly,
a ramp of ice magically formed, sloping
down to the ledge.

"Cool!" said Olaf. "Now she
can climb up to us!"

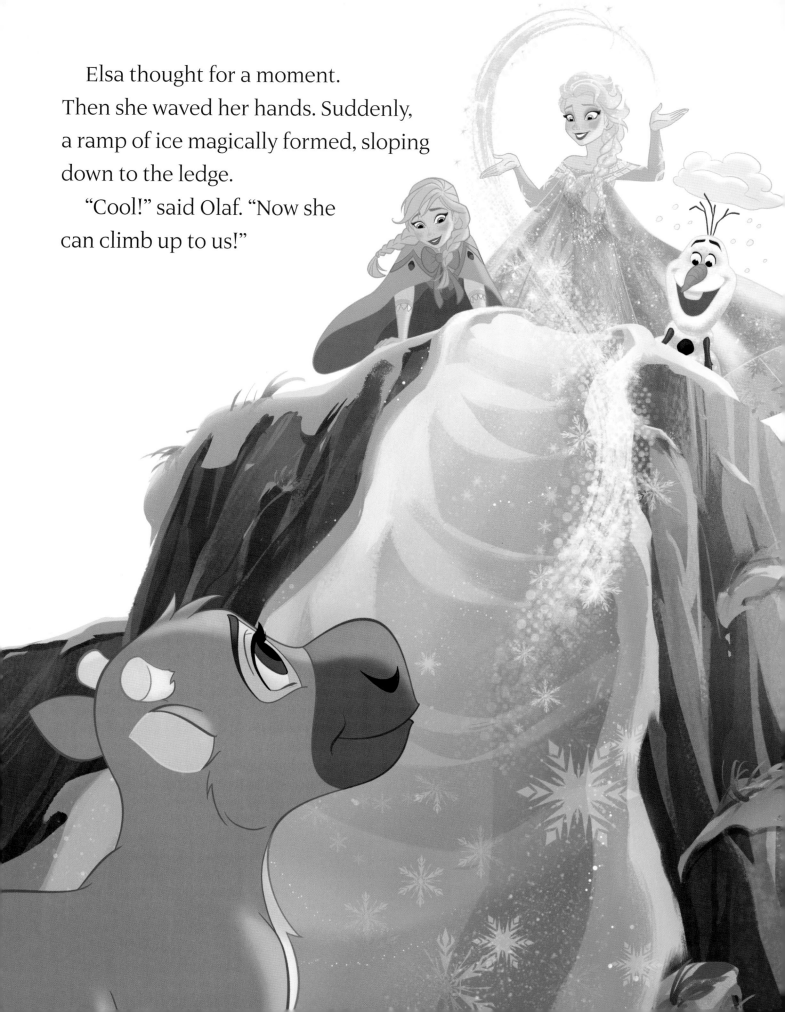

Carefully, the reindeer stepped
onto the ramp . . .

. . . but she fell right back down. The ice was too slippery!

"Now what?" asked Elsa.

"I know!" said Anna. She grabbed the supplies she had gotten from Oaken and slid down to the reindeer. "Hello, little one. Let's get you out of here."

First, Anna put the
snowshoes on the reindeer. "I knew
these would be useful," she said.
Then she threw a rope up to Elsa. "Pull!"
Anna shouted. Olaf helped, too.

Before long, everyone was safely back at the top!

"Can we invite the reindeer to the ball?" asked Olaf.

"The ball!" Anna and Elsa exclaimed together. They were going to be late!

Elsa pulled Anna and Olaf onto the cart. "Hold on!" she said. Using her magic, Elsa created a snow slide that led all the way down the mountain.

After an exciting ride, Elsa, Anna, Olaf, and the reindeer landed right in the middle of the ballroom! Crocuses rained down on the guests, who were delighted with the grand entrance.

"You did it!" Anna told her sister. "Nobody has ever seen a ball like this before!"

Elsa laughed. "And best of all, we're here together!"